TRIX
and
VIX

BY MARY AND CONRAD BUFF

HOUGHTON MIFFLIN COMPANY BOSTON

The Riverside Press Cambridge

TRIX AND VIX

TWO GRAY FOXES jumped down from the great limb of an old oak tree. They had been hiding all night in the tree from two dogs that had chased them from the valley below. As the vixen saw a deep hole at the base of the tree, she thought of her pups soon to be born. This deep dark hole would make a safe den.

The foxes carried oak leaves and shredded bark in their mouths to line the hole. It was now warm and soft. A short time later three blind, grayish fox pups were born in the den.

1

Since the father fox, or dog fox, could not enter the den until the babies were older, he hunted all night for them. He brought the vixen all kinds of game and laid it near the hole. Sometimes he caught a rabbit, or a field mouse, and often a wood rat. More often he brought fat ground squirrels to the family.

The vixen nursed her young pups and cared for them, and in a week their eyes opened. They began to play. They romped, tugged, and rolled about in the dark hole, growing stronger as each day passed.

Each one of the pups was different. One was a fearful fellow, always keeping close to mother and yelping. The second one was slower than her brothers. She was always behind them when they ventured from the den. Her name was Slowpoke. But the third pup was the strongest and quickest of the three. His name was Trix. He explored everything and went everywhere. He was sometimes TOO daring.

Once he saw a black and white animal waddling slowly toward him. He blocked her way and stared at her. She waved her long black and white tail. That was a warning to get out of her way. But Trix did not know that. She stamped her front feet. Still Trix stared at her. Now the skunk was really angry. Her little eyes grew red.

Suddenly she whirled like a top. Trix felt liquid fire sprayed into his eyes. He stumbled away, blinded for the moment and howling with pain. When he found his mother she chased him away. He smelled so bad he slept alone outside the den that night.

Trix never forgot his first skunk and after that let all skunks, big or little, alone.

4

All of the time Trix had been growing up, he had sniffed strange smells floating into the hills from the valley below. A great city lay spread out there for miles. Mother and Father Fox had not liked the smell of the city or the sounds of the city. They knew dogs lived there, and men with guns. But Trix was young and curious. Now that he was alone, he set out to explore the smells and sounds that came from the city below.

He wandered down a faint old trail that the deer used, now and then stopping to hunt. As he came lower in the hills, he heard dogs barking. He passed a few houses. He smelled humans. He heard humans. Sometimes he was about to turn back to his old home, but curiosity urged him on. He just HAD to find out.

It was dark. Suddenly he heard the sound of something rushing along a road nearby. He hid in a thicket. He saw two of the biggest and brightest eyes he had ever seen. The eyes were so fierce. A huge monster. Was he to be eaten up by this monster? The monster shrieked. Then suddenly it was gone, leaving only a vile odor. The two tiny red eyes at its rear vanished. Trix had seen his first automobile.

The frightened fox rushed across the road, and leaped into a canyon that smelled of greenness and water. He hid under a flat rock until his heart was more quiet. Under the rock was a den of field mice. He snapped them up, then curled in a ball and went to sleep. He slept until the next afternoon, for he was worn out with the new sights and sounds of the city.

When Trix awoke, he heard the whistle of a ground squirrel. Then the whirr of a quail. A jaybird screamed. Trix squirmed from under the rock. He was in a narrow canyon. At the bottom he found a pool of water. Near it dozed a fat frog. Trix caught the frog before it awoke. Dogs barked far away. He heard the sound of monsters like the one he had met one night racing along the road.

Again it was dark, and time to hunt. A delicious odor drifted down from the sky. Trix had never smelled anything so good. It was mingled with the smell of humans. The gray fox sneaked upward through the dense brush and came to a house on the rim of the canyon. Hiding in the bushes he peered into the house. It was all glass on one side. Two small humans were playing on the floor. He and his brother and sister had played like that when they were little. The wonderful odor came from the house. It was stronger now and made his mouth water.

Trix was so hungry that he dared to step out into the light for a moment.   One of the little humans saw him.

"Daddy, look, there's a puppy out in the garden.   Look."

A deeper voice replied, "Not a puppy, David, that's a gray fox.   The first time I ever saw a fox in the city."

Trix had never heard a human speak before.   He slunk away and hid in the shadows.   Yet the good smells kept him close to the house.

After the lights went out in the house, and it was dark, he crept back. He sniffed at doors. He listened. He heard humans softly breathing as they slept. He smelled the quiet monster in the garage. Its eyes were closed. It was asleep too.

Wandering around the garden, Trix found a pan of raisins. He gobbled them up as fast as he could. How delicious they were. He had never tasted anything like them. All at once, a strange animal climbed up from the canyon into the garden. It was almost as big as he was. It had a long tail like a rat. It was an opossum. The opossum looked at Trix. Trix stared at the opossum. Since the raisins were gone, there was nothing to fight over. After sniffing about, the opossum disappeared.

In the moonlight Trix explored other gardens. He found
a fishpond but a greedy raccoon was standing in the water
catching fish with his long delicate fingers. A dog barked
and Trix raced away. The raccoon climbed a nearby tree.

So began a new life for Trix, the curious fox. Each
evening, when dusk came, he sneaked up through the
tangled brush to the House of Good Smells and hid in the
shadow of the bushes. A glass door would rumble on its

17

track. A pan of food would be placed on the ground. Then the glass door would close with a thud. Only then would Trix dash out into the light, grab a raisin or a cookie or a piece of bread, and dash back into the shadow of the bushes. Other animals soon learned that they could eat well at the House of Good Smells. But Trix learned too that they came only when it was night. So he often waited at dusk, and being earlier, he usually finished the raisins or grapes before the others came. He grew fat and glossy.

As night followed night, Trix began to trust the humans that lived in the House of Good Smells. He would sit on the terrace like a hungry dog and listen for the children's voices. Then David or Jane would open the door and call, "Gray Fox, come here, raisins tonight. Come on, Gray Fox. We won't hurt you."

And, as they never made a quick movement to frighten him, or a sudden shout, he trusted them. This happy friendship might have gone on for a long time, but a family moved nearby and brought a police dog with them.

One night, when David and Jane were not at home, Trix came as usual for food. The wind was blowing that night, and the trees made frightening sounds. Trix was nervous. As he was nibbling on raisins, around the house dashed the big dog. He came so fast that Trix hardly had time to dodge and dash down the hill through the dense brush. He was very frightened.

Later that night he heard a large animal searching in the brush and that made him more afraid. Would the police dog come every night now? Would the dog find his den some evening and kill him? Trix wondered if he should go back to the hills where he was born. It was safe there. He might find his mother or his brother. Before dawn Trix had made up his mind. He MUST go back.

Hurriedly he crossed the road, loped up the faint trail, and soon left cars, humans, smells, dogs, far far behind him. He came at last to the old oak tree where he was born. A family of skunks now lived in the old den. He had never liked skunks, big or little, so he wandered on.

For a long time Trix searched in the hills for his family. Often he was lonely. He could not find his mother or brother. He hunted, as usual, for ground squirrels, quail, rabbits and gophers. He went higher up into the mountains among the evergreens and found juniper berries. He liked juniper berries, but not as much as raisins.

It was colder now. An early snow fell. Trix had never seen snow and did not like it. He searched for a warm shelter. Finding one under a rock, he crawled inside. From deep within came a low growl. He had crawled into a fox den. But this fox was friendly. She was about his age, and alone too. She was smaller than Trix and beautiful. Her name was Vix.

Since both Trix and Vix had been alone for so long it was good to have a friend to hunt with. But mice and ground squirrels had gone to sleep in their burrows deep in the earth. The snow rabbits had turned white and were hard to catch. The wind blew and made strange sounds among the pines. The foxes were cold and always hungry.

While the two foxes were hunting in the snow of the mountains, down in the city below, Jane and David waited and waited for their gray fox to come. Where had he gone? Why did he not come back at night any more?

They did not know that the police dog had frightened him away, for they were not at home the night the dog had chased Trix.

Each evening David and Jane put out grapes, or cookies, or bread, or raisins for Trix and called, "Gray Fox, come, Gray Fox, we won't hurt you."

But Trix never came.   In the morning the food was gone. Raccoons, skunks, or opossums had eaten it, not Trix.

Each morning the children asked, "Daddy, do you think Gray Fox will come tonight?"

Their father would shake his head sadly and reply, "I don't know.   Perhaps the cars drove him away, or people. The city is not the place for foxes.   All we can do is wait and hope.   He may come back some evening, and stand right there on the terrace, waiting for you."

So Jane and David waited. Then one evening their
father brought home a newspaper. On the front page was
a picture of a ten-year-old boy of the neighborhood. He
held a dead fox by its beautiful long tail. In the other
hand he had a bow. He had shot the fox with an arrow
and seemed very proud of himself.

When the children saw the picture they cried, "Is that OUR fox? It looks just like him. He had a beautiful long tail. That mean old boy—why did he go and shoot our friend? Foxes don't hurt anybody. They just eat up mice and rats. Is it our fox, Daddy?"

"Foxes look alike," their father said. "It may not be OUR fox at all. Some men and boys just love to kill anything living. I telephoned the Humane Society to find out if they had caught a fox recently. They said no. But if they had, they would have taken it up to the hills and let it go free. That is, if it was healthy. Let us hope Gray Fox is roaming the mountains FREE right now."

Trix and Vix WERE roaming the mountains free, but it was cold and they were often hungry. The snow did not melt. Gradually they drifted downward with the deer

toward the warmer lowlands. One night they came to the old oak tree where Trix was born. But the skunks were still there, so Trix passed by without stopping. Vix now followed him wherever he went. Finally the two foxes came to the little canyon where Trix had spent happy times. Trix showed his friend the den under the flat rock. It was empty now though it smelled faintly of raccoon.

That evening Trix sneaked up through the dense brush and hid in the shadow of a bush near the House of Good Smells. Vix crept after him and hid too. They could see into the house. Jane and David were sitting on the floor, looking at a book. When David laughed, Vix was frightened. She had never heard a human laugh before. Far away a dog barked. But it was a small dog. Trix was not afraid.

He was hungry. He walked into the light and stood there waiting, as beautiful as ever, his long glossy tail flowing behind him, his bright eyes eager. David saw him.

"Mother, Daddy, there's Gray Fox."

They all looked. It WAS their fox. Only their fox would have stood so quietly in the light waiting for the door to open and the children to call.

Jane ran to the kitchen. Yesterday she had had a birthday party and one piece of her cake was left. She opened the door and laid the cake down on the bricks, calling, "Gray Fox, here's my birthday cake. I am eight now."

Trix hardly waited for the door to close before he grabbed a hunk of the cake. Then he thought of Vix. He took another bite and melted into the shadow of the bushes. Vix smelled the cake and grabbed it from him. Then she peeked out of the shadow for only a moment, but the children saw her lovely little head.

"Look, there's another fox, a smaller one. Gray Fox gave her a piece of the cake. She's his friend."

Father and Mother smiled.

"Maybe that's why our fox went away, to get his friend."

The children jumped for joy.

"She's smaller than he is," said Jane. "Do you think she's a vixen, Daddy?"

"She may be," answered Father.

Then Jane looked up at her mother, a question in her eyes. "Mother, do you think SOMETIME our foxes will have babies?"

"They might," answered Mother.

"Then, Mother," again asked Jane, her eyes shining, "if they DO have babies, do you think they might bring them up here so we can see them? Of course when they're big enough."

"It could happen," answered Mother, smiling.

"Of course, it COULD happen," added Father hopefully.

"It COULD happen," whispered Jane to David.

AND IT DID HAPPEN